MRS LEAR

Laura Kalpakian

SHORTLIST

First published in 2013 by
AudioGO Ltd
by arrangement with
the Author

ISBN 978 1 4713 2652 3

British Library Cataloguing in Publication Data available

Printed and bound in Great Britain by TJ International
Limited

I know many of these people. I have probably slept with some of the men at one time or another (none of them experiences I care to repeat, or even remember) so when they smile in a way meant to be flattering at my age, I nod, turn, and retreat into regal indifference. My name is called. The Dean asks the audience of some hundred people sitting at white-clad tables to welcome me, Audra Lear, 'A distinguished doyenne of Canadian theatre.' Polite applause ensues. The playwright, Gordon Freeman, at the head table, the most distinguished of everyone here (though he's also a distinguished shit and toady). The author of a dozen West End triumphs, Gordon is the luminary at the center of this conference, *Canadian Theatre in the 21st Century: A Symposium.* Ridiculous title. But what of it? Our expenses are paid, plus a nice honorarium. We are assembled for lunch in the long, sunlit dining room at the University of Guelph. The wine bottles, once emptied, are replaced, and the tables dotted with small vases of summer flowers. I sit down. As others are introduced to equally gentle applause, I play with my salad fork and think back. Doyenne? Distinguished? In truth my career reflects sheer stamina, good health, and not being too picky about parts or venues. Dinner theatre, fine, I'll do it. Mystery-in-the-round, fine. University summer stock, fine. Theatre cruises for the elderly? Fine. Repertory companies in the Yukon, fine. My youthful dreams have been realized; my voice has echoed in a thousand drafty provincial halls for the past half century. I, Audra Lear, I have a life in theatre! Some might say the theatre is a wretched, uncertain, impecunious life. Perhaps. Grim backstage, but gaudy on. Yes. But face it, a bright life, and much to be envied.

The purpose of this luncheon is so that all of us, distinguished professionals, might meet and bond before the actual conference begins. The thought is laughable. That many theatre people in one place? We are more likely to murder one another than bond. Sitting there at lunch, though, we did rather bond over the name tags they had given us, joked that the conference planners must be morons to give actors name tags. An actor's face *is* his name tag, and the poor sod who needs something pinned to his lapel might as well hang up his false beard. Like children determined to defeat obtuse adults, we all unpinned our name tags, and put them under our plates, laughed, and went on to enjoy the university's white wine, wilted greens and pale fish.

But conference planners are not so easily out-maneuvered. They had thick packets for each of us, and an afternoon's slate of after-lunch events. This included being escorted, in groups of a dozen or so, around the university's excellent dramatic facilities. These tours were led by good looking students who spoke to us in English and in French. Oh God, *Mon Dieu,* twice as long and tedious! I wanted to get off my aching feet, go back to the hotel room, have a cold beer, watch TV, sleep, anything but follow that bright-eyed student. But at my age, you can never let on that the years have made inroads on your stamina, or your feet. If I were young and sexy and in demand, I'd turn to the guide, and say *Ta-ta! I'm off! Tell the program director I am too fucking busy. Or vice versa*.

But part of the dreary herd, I followed our boring, bubbly guide through the innovative performance space and all its electronic marvels. On to the state-of-the-art costuming room where this twit rattles at bilingual length. Believe me, I wanted to tell her, all you really need is needle, thread, skilled hands and someone who can work quickly. She led us to the lifts that would carry us up to the sound and lighting booths. All very impressive. My feet are killing me.

At last we came to the Drama Library where the young lady proudly drew our attention to the most complete collcction of plays in all of Canada. Row upon row, shelf upon shelf, floor to ceiling, an entire room of plays, small bound books, unused, unspoken, unopened. What had once been voiced, now confined to covers and condemned to silence. It was like being in a mausoleum of the only half-dead. Perhaps it was the wine at lunch, or simple fatigue, or somehow the overripe accumulation of my years in the profession, but my head began to spin among all those plays with short lives and shrouded reputations, stale print on stale pages, stale names, and forgotten roles, short runs and unremembered lines. Oh, I have acted in thousands of such plays, have bled and expended my very soul into plays whose lines barely crossed the proscenium before they were yanked, and all that work for naught. And yet, who knows better than an actor that the function of the play is not immortality. The function of the play is to fill up the theatre with warm bodies who will applaud. If the seats aren't filled, if they don't applaud, your gnashing and thrashing, toil and trouble are for naught. The play is pulled and everyone is out of work. Albert Crudup's dictum, *The actor dies. The play turns to dust. The theatre endures,* famous for its cynicism—famous at least to anyone who knew the tyrannical old bastard—battered at my heart and mind and memory. I wanted to weep for all these small paper-bound volumes, these forgotten characters forever denied cues and curtain. I felt a great *for naught* of my whole life. I felt faint, my brain began to peel away from the inside of my skull, the sound like tearing silk.

'Excuse me,' said a finely cultivated voice at my back. 'May I offer you an arm?'

'I'm fine. It's nothing.'

'Aren't you Audra Lear?'

He was slim, dressed in a natty fashion, with a fine web of veins across his cheeks and carefully groomed eyebrows, younger than I, but I could not place him. And of course, he had no nametag. I basked a bit in his having recognized me and—it must be said—enjoyed a little frisson of pleasure when he asked me to have a drink with him later. However, it turned out that all he really wanted was an audition for the theatre cruise I was doing out of Vancouver directly after the conference. He said he too was from

Ottawa, as if that ought to endear him to me. Fat chance.

* * *

Ottawa is the capital city of a country full of people who best know what we are not. Defined in the negative. Canadians are not Americans, not British, not French, though our population hugs the American border, we ape the British and speak French. O Canada, who art thou? Perhaps fittingly, I am Canadian. Before I was delivered into the theatre, my very life could be expressed in negatives. No especial beauty. No discernable talents. A conscientious student, child of regular habits and inculcated routines.

My father, Thomas Fox, managed a gentlemen's haberdashery. He kept regular hours. Our large, comfortable apartment was on the second floor of a duplex with a stoop fronting a street of other buildings just like it. In back there was a prickly scrap of lawn (white in winter, beige in summer) and a view of backs of dun-colored brick buildings just like ours. Our windows were curtained in velvet to keep out the cold (and the light). The bedroom doors were kept closed, and so the hall was dark even on the brightest day. Nothing was modern. Even the radio, and later the TV, looked like antique fetishes with knobs. Sideboards and beds and bureaus, overstuffed chairs, all were weighty, old, inherited, mostly from Mother's family (who, she was fond of saying, had been Canadian for generations). Heaviest of all were the ornate frames around the bevy of family pictures: little girls in be-ribboned frocks, scowling boys, toothless grannies with solemn old husbands, long ago wedding portraits, widows in weeds, wistful young women, men in the uniform of bygone conflicts. My family were, on both sides, an upright, colorless lot, right down to rich tubercular Aunt Audra for whom I was named in hopes she would leave me her money. (She didn't.)

* * *

As a girl I accompanied my parents, and stood with knots of mourners at wind-swept cemeteries saying farewell. There were lots of funerals. My family hadn't any talent or tenacity for life. My relatives reminded me of retail clothing, all the same, only in different sizes. All hanging on the rack, lifeless, without warmth or animation. When we returned home, Mother would go through the house and find any heavy framed picture that included the Late Lamented, and turn it to the wall for forty days. Mother's version of mourning. And then, forty days later she turned their pictures back around, behold! They looked almost cheerful, as though they had been refreshed by dying.

As a child I feared the pictures in the hall and dining room. I tiptoed past them, believing they meant me harm. I had nightmares that they would ooze or leap from their dark frames and fall upon me, bury me in their dim lives. The pictures lining the hall were the worst since I walked that hall every day. The pictures in the dining room I could avoid, except when Mother obliged me to dust weekly. Otherwise, we never used the dark dining room, save perhaps for Christmas and Thanksgiving.

We were just three. My mother and father and I took our dreary meals at the kitchen table. The table was always laid for breakfast the night before, so to reassure ourselves that tomorrow would indeed be exactly like today. Except when Cousin Susan lived with us, the dishrack beside the sink held always three of everything, one teapot, and whatever my mother used to cook in. Whatever she cooked tasted like leather or laundry. Still, we bowed daily our heads and said our prayers over these meals, my parents giving me to understand that I was fortunate to be a Canadian child, safe, and warm, and well fed, and not some poor English child, or European living in want, devastated by war.

These were not idle admonitions. My schooldays were spent in the wake of the Second World War, and in the shadow of those upheavals. My favorite teacher was the inspiring Miss Toth, young, histrionic and passionate. She fired our pubescent hearts and ignited conviction in our narrow little minds. This was perhaps '47, '48, and Miss Toth (whose sweetheart had perished in North Africa) exhorted us to be forever grateful to the British military and to our own Canadian and Anzac troops (never mind the

Americans' late entry, and the less said of the French, the better) that Herr Hitler's picture was not on our classroom wall instead of the King's. Think about that! Sprechen sie Deutsches? Think about that! She told fierce tales of the Blitz, and British suffering, of cities laid waste, smoking rubble, firebombs hurling out of the night skies. The whistle and shriek and thud before the explosions. Families sleeping, living deep in the bowels of the earth while overhead bombs burst and the deep Tube tunnels shook. Emerging only to find their street bombed, their homes destroyed. Miss Toth filled us with empathy when she spoke of the gallant British people, of the Want and Fear that reigned over their lives in wartime. Coal and bacon and butter and sugar, eggs and meat all severely rationed, the deprivation felt by all. That ham sandwich in your lunch, Miss Toth told us gravely, that sandwich would be *a feast* for some poor British child. When I heard these words, I would have given that ham sandwich to the mice.

But the best part of Miss Toth's performance (for that's what it was; I see it now) was reserved for our personal mission, that is, Canada's mission. She urged us to see the recent flux of immigrants to our shores as a League of Survivors (her phrase). O Canada had a special role. We must succor the orphan, lift the mantle of grief from the widow, assuage want, protect and sustain these refugees. Let other nations refer to the emigrant as FOB. Let other nations look down on those souls who sought shelter. Our Canadian strength is equal to this noble task in this brave, new postwar world. On a signal from Miss Toth, we stood, faced the flag, sang the national anthem, all of us afire with empathy and zeal.

It's true that in these years Canada

absorbed a great influx of people, different races and countries and faiths, the very people who now render our cities wonderfully cosmopolitan. But at the time, as Miss Toth clearly knew, these people, were a source of chagrin. They often smelled bad, and brought with them the unmistakable, un-wash-off-able aura of people crowded, herded, crouching for generations. How could they hope to fit into a land of vast prairies and rocky coasts, mountains ranges, frozen tundra and majestic waterways?

With Miss Toth's eloquence ringing in my ears, I came home one afternoon to find my mother with a visitor at the kitchen table, tea laid before them. My mother introduced her as Cousin Susan Butterfield. Mother and Cousin Susan had never actually met, though they knew of one another, naturally. Mother had already showed Cousin Susan the picture in the dining room, a heavy-framed family picture taken in Coventry, summer 1890, where all the girls wore sweet frocks. Susan's mother and Mother's mother, cousins, stood side by side in this picture. That may be, I thought to myself, but I could see no family resemblance at all.

Fortyish, or possible older. (Or possibly younger; you couldn't tell.) Susan was pale, with a soft doughy complexion, dull brown hair going gray, very long and pulled into a slipshod bun. Dandruff dusted the shoulders of the dark broadcloth traveling suit that shapelessly encased her. She had bright blue eyes, but she kept her head tucked down, like a bird looking to put its head under its wing. Old perspiration smells wafted from her. She hardly spoke and when she did, her voice was soft and unused; the words formed slowly, as though she must make a pact with each one before she would part with it. Her bad teeth looked like a little graveyard, the headstones all rotting and askew. Her tongue lolled out by the side of her mouth like a small reliable pet. Beside her chair there was a cardboard suitcase and beside that an overstuffed bag from which I could just see peeking a roll of toilet paper.

Cousin Susan had just arrived in Ottawa, said Mother. Just arrived in Canada. Or very lately, yes? Mother paused and looked at Susan expectantly, but she only nodded. Mother said she wished she'd known Cousin Susan was coming and we could have been better prepared. Mother went on about Coventry, long ago, where their mothers were cousins, telling her favorite, fine old boring anecdotes, and pouring more tea. Mother and Susan both sighed over Coventry's fate, bombed to bits during the War.

Clearing her throat several times,

and in a rusty voice, Susan said, 'I left Coventry.' Cousin Susan studied her teacup, lifted it from its saucer and put it on the table. She turned the saucer over and pointed to the word printed on the bottom. *Staffordshire.* 'I came from Staffordshire.'

Mother continued with inconsequential chatter, pouring more tea. Susan heaped sugar into the cup, six, maybe seven spoonfuls of sugar. You'd think the spoon would stand up by itself. Her face twitching, her tongue lolling happily, she looked all around the tiny kitchen, sighing, 'So lovely. Everything is so very lovely.'

'Yes, well you did well to come to Canada,' said Mother, sounding very like Miss Toth. 'My grandfather and his brother came in 1905. We have been Canadian for generations. More tea? Another biscuit?'

Susan took three, dropped two into her lap, keeping one hand over them protectively. With her other hand she shoved the other into her mouth, little crumbs flying from her open lips. She chewed contentedly while Mother kept talking, though you could see she was appalled. Suddenly Susan interrupted Mother, and said she had to use the toilet. Said it just like that, too. Toilet.

Mother colored slightly and directed her to the lavatory. Cousin Susan excused herself, and when she walked, she scurried, as though pursued by gnats.

We heard the toilet chain pull, and the hot water pipes rattled repeatedly. Mother ventured to hope Susan was taking a bath. Under the spell of Miss Toth, I told mother that Cousin Susan was one of the League of Survivors and couldn't help the way she smelled.

The very next day I proudly informed Miss Toth that my parents had risen to her high standards. The Fox family would shelter Cousin Susan till she could find work. We only had the two bedrooms, and so they gave Susan my bed, and Mother made up a pallet on the floor for me. But Cousin Susan would not let me sleep there. From that very first night, she insisted on the pallet. With few words, mostly grimaces and gestures, her head bobbing up and down, she insisted on the pallet for herself, gave me to understand she preferred it.

So, guilt-ridden, I got in my own bed. I turned out the bedside lamp. 'Are you sure, Susan?'

'Yes.'

Perhaps twenty minutes passed, and then her dry voice unfurled slowly. 'A story, Audra? Tell a story?'

'I don't know any. Do you?'

'Oh yes.' She rolled up tightly, facing the wall.

'But I am sworn to secrecy.'

Her secrecy slowly unraveled in the three weeks we shared my room, whispering in the dark. I learned that Susan had no one left. Her sweetheart died at Dunkirk. One brother in Burma. Another in North Africa. Her father perished in one of the Coventry factories bombed to bits in 1940; her younger sister and the family home were destroyed in the firestorm that followed. Susan and her mother, homeless and destitute, were moved to a tiny bedsit in a suburb unfamiliar to them. Here, Susan's mother died of a broken heart, a slow suicide, refusing all food. Susan was broken-hearted, alone and desperate, but she vowed to herself when the war ended, she would build a new life. For all her eccentricities, her snores and farts, I admired her. After all, though neither young nor handsome, nor especially intelligent, still she'd shown considerable courage in leaving Britain for an uncertain welcome with a distant cousin in Canada. To me she exemplified the League of Survivors. The two of us, refugee and teenage girl, we struck a peculiar alliance.

Every day after lunch Susan put on her coat and hat and took the newspaper with promising jobs circled. She got on the bus and returned empty handed in time for tea. The good jobs all went to men anyway, and she had no useful skills. Yes, she was literate; she could do sums and the like, but she couldn't type or take shorthand. She was so loathe to speak, she couldn't even have answered telephones. With her tongue-lolling and head-bobbing she couldn't get any job where she had to interact with the public. She sewed a fine hand, as the old nursery rhyme has it, a wizard with a needle and thread. But fancy needlework? Can you think of a more antiquated ability in a go-ahead place like Ottawa? My father's haberdashery firm could not even hire her as a seamstress, despite her skills; she was too bizarre to be around gentlemen.

The bucket and a mop, that's all that's left to her. Susan bestirred herself daily, every morning, around our house, cleaning, mopping, swabbing out sinks, the tub, the toilet, making beds, vacuuming, dusting, washing up, all the laundry and ironing, including my father's shirts starched just the way he liked. She freed Mother from all housework save for the cooking. Such as it was. She did this without ever once, as far as I know, being asked, or thanked.

Nor did she complain when my parents moved her pallet out of my room and to the floor of the unused dining room. Servants quarters, in a manner of speaking. She slept there beneath the family pictures, including the 1890 one of her mother in the be-ribboned frock. When she had a bad dream, there were no screams or cries, but in the mornings we would find her in the corner, the dining room lights blazing away, as she clutched her knees, and bit her tongue as it quivered outside her lips. But for the most part, Susan was silent and collected. She took a bath religiously, every Thursday. She heaped her tea with sugar. She grew chubby. On Sundays Susan stayed home and read the funny papers while we three went to church. On Sunday evenings my parents attended church board meetings, leaving me and Susan to enjoy companionable Sunday suppers together. I grew accustomed to her odd little rituals. I knew the War had done this to her, the Blitz and bombing, but the war was years ago, and watching her clutch half empty toilet rolls to her bosom, or shove them up her nightgown sleeves and bolt for the dining room, seemed to me merely comic, pathetic.

Still, fired with Miss Toth's zeal for the League of Survivors (and though Susan never once complained) I burned with shame at her treatment.

One evening in a fit of histrionic indignation, I faced my parents in the sitting room, and denounced them for treating Susan like a slavey, for taking advantage of her simple wish to please. My father said Susan was indeed a relative, but not a guest. Susan was working off her debt. Room and board. He said he gave her wages. I thought he was lying, but I did not dare challenge him. With my little impassioned snit finished (my first great performance in retrospect) I left the room.

Perhaps fourteen such months passed, and then Susan found a miraculous job for her antique skills. She was taken on provisionally as under-assistant to the wardrobe mistress at that great old theatre, the Odéon, built in 1912 with all the splendor and extravagance of overblown Edwardian glamour. Susan Butterfield, the mute, middle-aged orphan with dandruff and bad teeth was cast headlong into the theatre! A world both brilliant and foreign.

My parents were pleased. They saw less of her and she paid reliable rent, weekly, cash money left on the kitchen table. Having a job also softened her eccentric edges. She cut her gray hair very short, like a little tight cap around her skull, and this accentuated her luminous blue eyes, further enlarged when she began wearing glasses. Her scurrying walk slowed, though she remained afflicted with her little tics and grimaces, unable to carry on a proper conversation. Father had long since quit speaking to her at all, and Mother addressed her only to enumerate household tasks. Other than that, they ignored her. Except for those Sunday evening suppers with me, Susan took all her meals alone. She ate over the kitchen sink, facing the window, her back to the rest of the room. She always wrapped some little morsel in a napkin, and tucked it in her pocket.

Susan worked six nights a week at the Odéon, as well as the Saturday matinee, so Saturdays she was gone all day. (Sundays the theatre was closed because Albert Crudup, the tyrannical owner, was devoutly religious.) Theatrical hours, yes, but by Fox family standards she came home very late, and she got up very late. Mother found Susan's sleeping till noon all but intolerable. Moreover, weeknights, Susan went to work when normal offices were closing up. My father would sometimes pass her on the stairs as he was coming home from the haberdashery. He claimed that Susan's weird hours were having a bad effect on his health. He simply couldn't sleep knowing that someone would open our front door after midnight even if she had a key. Still, the cash Susan paid weekly and the housework she performed daily, these were not to be scorned, and she stayed on with us for three years and eight months.

After Susan went to work at the Odéon, our Sunday suppers became exciting. In what for her was a torrent of words (her eyebrows jumping all over, mouth twisting, tongue trembling, nose wrinkling, eyes rolling) Susan waxed on about her life backstage: waiting in the wings, watching every performance, her arms banded with pincushions, her apron pockets stocked with tools, scissors and supplies, her needles all threaded, ready for any emergency, for some over-zealous Lady of the Camellias say, fleeing her lover while he still had his foot on her train. Susan thrilled to everything. The plays and actors and costumes! She had never, before the Odéon, been to a theatre. Oh the music hall, yes, often with dear Will (the sweetheart dead at Dunkirk) and after he died, with the neighbor boy. (He also died.) But the theatre? In her wisp of her voice, she said, 'Oh, Audra, the magic of it! You have no idea.'

And it was true, I had no idea. My family never went to the theatre. We seldom went to films. That old darkened magic that descends in that moment between the lights dimming and the curtain rising? I never experienced that. My family had no use for fictions of any sort. The few novels in our house were of the sturdy, Christian-virtue variety, *Ben-Hur, Quo Vadis,* and the like. Poetry? There might have been a volume of Milton, and perhaps a book of Browning or *Idylls of the King*. But no one read them. My parents read the newspaper, daily, beginning to end. The sound of a rustling newsprint to this day gives me a fleeting, intense claustrophobic cramp in the mind. My parents did without the magic of make-believe and never felt the loss of it. Nor did I, until Cousin Susan began working at the Odéon, and adolescence filled me with that odd, unstable brew of yearning and resentment. My teachers after Miss Toth were grim and dull. School, even my friends seemed narrow, boring. I longed for inspiration, and though Susan herself was hardly inspiring, the life she spoke of was magical, beckoning, and beautiful. How very extraordinary to think that this job of Susan's was the single most fundamental event of my entire life. What might I have otherwise been? I can't even imagine.

*   *   *

By the time I was fifteen Susan had made herself indispensable to the Odéon. So competent and at-the-ready was Susan Butterfield that the wardrobe mistress and her regular assistant soused themselves nightly into a happy stupor, and neither Albert Crudup, the fierce puritanical owner, nor Walter Jenkins, the steely stage manager, need ever know. Susan would certainly never tell, never complain for that matter. But Albert Crudup was no fool. He figured out that he did not need to pay three sets of wages for what Susan was doing alone. He fired the two tipplers. Weird Susan Butterfield became the Odéon wardrobe mistress; she was skilled, and equal to any task obliged of her. But the burden of doing the work of three placed a strain on her. I convinced her I could be her apprentice, at least for the Saturday matinees. She agreed, but she insisted I get Mother's permission. Susan was afraid of Mother.

Permission was refused, indeed, refused with a snort of disbelief, wondering what sorts of bizarre ideas Cousin Susan had put in my head. I did not tell her the ideas were mine. I was determined to have my way. To be in the League of Survivors you had to be more than brave or stalwart, you had to be clever too. I told Susan I was going to lie, and she gave a philosophical tic, as though to say, *Of course you will lie! What else would you do?*

I told Mother I was taking the bus and meeting other girls at the library to study every Saturday afternoon. Delivering this bit of fiction with conviction and panache was my second great performance. I always did well in school, so Saturday studying at the library was not impossible or even unlikely. I'd never given my mother reason to distrust me, and she probably would have thought such a bald lie beyond my imagination. Certainly it was beyond hers.

I was never one of those actresses whose inspiration comes first from being in the audience, a girl enchanted by the play. I knew my calling from the wings. These Saturday afternoons were for me, a baptism, total immersion: the dark wings, the flats, the high flies disappearing to the gloom, the gas and lighting men, the sweating scene shifters, the creaking pulleys, the smell of bad drains and damp passages and old velvet and cigarette smoke, though signs everywhere forbade smoking. There were grimy windows at street level that gave on to dressing rooms festooned with laundry, and their cocktail of odors: perspiration, perfume, smoke, make up, re-heated coffee, spilled tea, and burnt hair from the curling tongs used on wigs. Everyone shared dressing rooms, save for the most illustrious of actors. The bathrooms smelled of cold porcelain and old urine; they sounded with the cacophony of hissing radiators and banging pipes. In the windowless green room there were lumpy chairs and couches, scarred tables where candy wrappers sometimes smouldered in overflowing ash trays. There was an air of comradely rot, apple cores and orange peels drying, sandwich ends withering, beer going stale in bottles and milk going bad somewhere out of sight. The actresses bickered and sniped as they plucked their eyebrows, while the actors preened like rare, ugly birds. The stage manager, Walter Jenkins, was a fussy, bullying sort. And Albert Crudup, owner-manager of the Odéon? Shrewd, and rude and strait-laced, Albert Crudup was God.

Albert Crudup was gaunt, hawk-like, with scant gray hair and bushy eyebrows. His cigarette, sometimes lit, sometimes not, was always between his teeth. He wore shirtsleeves, and only ever put on a coat and tie if he were going to venture into the House, to sit there with the audience and judge their responses. He bristled rectitude, detested smut and scandal. It was rumored that on the Sabbath he read nothing but the Bible. Certainly Mrs. Crudup never came to the theatre, nor did his children, except when Shaw was on the bill. Even Shakespeare had too much sex and raunchy innuendo for their tender sensibilities.

With the actors though, Albert Crudup was merciless. The Odéon was never dark, one play followed another. Mr. Crudup could see, sense, the first whiff of failure for a play. That's when he started rehearsal on another. His repertory actors were not paid for rehearsals. They dared not complain. They would rehearse the new play all afternoon, then perform that night in the doomed play. Life, as under any tyrant, was simple: If you didn't cross Mr. Crudup, you worked. If you once crossed him, you were finished. For Albert Crudup actors were entirely dispensable. He played them as one would cards in a game of poker. Any actor who proved himself no longer useful got tossed out.

I watched. I learned. I understood, even from my lowly station as

Susan's assistant, that to be an actor was to join the fraternity of those who want nothing else but to be feel the boards beneath their feet, footlights before them, painted flats at their backs. I kept my hopes and dreams, my acting aspirations and secret ambitions absolutely to myself. Too precious, too close to my soul to share with anyone. Anyway, whom could I tell? My parents? Perish the thought. Susan Butterfield? Susan would not have told anyone (after all, she hardly spoke, and even then, her communications were mostly twitching bits of gibberish) but she could not possibly comprehend the depth of my ambition. As for girlish, giggling confidences with my friends? Not even tempting. School was but a dream from which I woke on Saturdays. What I, young Audra Fox, felt was like a religious calling, not as if I wanted to be a nun, but as if I wanted to be a saint. I took secret vows. The theatre was my monastic order, and I obeyed its rules, however aberrant they might look to the outside world. I lived for Saturday to serve the church as acolyte, novice, postulant, even martyr.

Now, as an old woman, after more than fifty years on stage, I have regrets. Who does not? I, Audra Lear, have had my moments of madness on the midnight heath, my moments of glad grace. I have never been married to the king, but I have slept with the fool. More than one, alas. I do not flatter myself that I have created art. Theatre is much more about artifice than art. Art may be practiced singularly. Artifice is achieved collectively. Acting is a communal life; one lives and breathes and has one's being (to say nothing of eating, peeing, sleeping) in the intimate company of like-minded others. The magic of the theatre is only achieved by unflagging, repetitive work.

Theatrical people don't want to be preening and posing and wondering how Art might be served. They want to be working. Albert Crudup always said *Art should hang itself—and charge admission*.

His other favorite dictum he used, on every possible occasion, to remind everyone of their professional mortality. *The play dissolves. The actor dies. Only the theatre endures*. There was never any murky regret in his voice. On the contrary, he seemed rather cheered to remind us all how we depended on him. At the Odéon, the play's the thing, and we all served it. And Him. Albert Crudup was God and we were mortal.

I was completely accepted as Susan's informal assistant. I say informal because I was not paid. No one thought of paying me. No one really thought of me at all. No longer a child, neither was I a woman, only a long-legged, fair-skinned girl, with lank brown hair and blue eyes. No beauty, but smart, quick, useful and not underfoot. I became adept with a needle myself, a skill that has served me well in my own long career. I was careful to remain unobtrusive as is humanly possible, and careful not to trespass on the actors' (very limited) tolerance. I lived in fear of Mr. Crudup and Walter Jenkins, the stage manager, afraid they would look too closely, see how young I was, and banish me. But no one ever asked my age. Susan and I worked well together because I understood her strange tics, the small, sharp gestures that were a sort of nervous shorthand. Every Saturday I stood with her in the wings, ready to respond. Now and then, when I rose quickly to some small emergency, she eked an approving gape-mouthed smile, her tongue resting comfortably at the corner like a contented pink cat.

Before long I noticed Susan had

added a bit of lace at the collar, or a ruffle at the wrist of her black, dun and gray clothes. There was a man in her life, Fred Holliwell, an Odéon stagehand. There wasn't any banter between them, no fluttering eyelashes. No coy remonstrance. Probably I alone noticed their connection, and I noticed because Fred Holliwell often stood too close to Susan and she did not move away. Ordinarily Susan never let anyone too close to her, except perhaps for me.

Now with a beau and a job, Susan was no longer simply a stricken, middle-aged orphan, though she remained eccentric, at least at home. No doubt she would have been less so if she didn't sleep beneath those grim portraits of the austere dead in their be-ribboned frocks. Her little rituals were weird and could not be upset. She drank her tea not from a cup, but from a stout jam jar, and then hid it under the sink. She saved all the bacon drippings from her breakfasts and kept them in a little can on the kitchen windowsill. Periodically Mother would throw these cans away when they started to smell, or when she found a fly happily dying in the fat. When Susan found her can of grease gone, she cried and keened. She curled herself on the pallet on the dining room floor and wailed piteously. The whole building heard her. Probably the whole neighborhood. It was eerie and terrible. I could no longer think of her as one of the League of Survivors, but I remained her ally at home, defending her against my parents who were ongoingly unjust.

That last Christmas she lived with us, Susan brought home a box with a ribbon, a gift probably from Fred, but when my father asked her outright, she would not say. The gift was a flesh colored pink chenille robe and she loved it. She took to wandering around the house in this, loosely tied over less-than-fresh linen. (The expression was Mother's.) Susan ate her lonely breakfast in this robe. She did the mop and bucket brigade in this robe, and it would sometimes fall open when she bent over, especially when she bent over to fling the bucket contents out the back. The old man who lived across the way loved it. Mother saw him grinning in his window, actually bouncing up and down with excitement, and pointing to his happy, naked erection.

Mother was horrified, and reprimanded Susan sharply. Susan only said he was an old man after all. He had seen it all before. And even if he hadn't, what harm could there be? He was an old man. This was a very long speech for Susan.

Mother informed Father she wanted that slattern, that wanton Cousin Susan, out of our house, rent or no rent, and Father gave her a week's notice, but she was gone the next day. I came home from school to find Susan, her suitcase and pallet gone, and Mother in the dining room, making little disgusted exclamations over Susan's detritus. Mother would have to clean it up herself. She was too embarrassed to let anyone else do it. My parents never saw Cousin Susan again. And clearly they believed my association with her had ended as well.

But Susan and I still saw each other every Saturday. She made no mention of her moving out, and cast no aspersions on my parents. When I said I thought they were terrible and unfair, she shrugged. She didn't say where she had moved to, and I didn't ask. I wasn't even really curious. All that mattered to me was that my Saturdays at the Odéon should continue.

Later, after the disaster, I wrote Susan a groveling letter of apology, and only then did I realize I had no address for her. I put my abject letter, four hand-scrawled pages, in an envelope and addressed it to Miss Susan Butterfield c/o the Odéon. It was returned to me, refused. *Addressee unknown* stamped over Susan's name. Had Susan refused it? I don't know. Or had Mr. Crudup dismissed her in retaliation for my disaster? That too, I do not know. She had, for all intents and purposes, vanished.

When this letter was returned to sender—that is, me, Miss Audra Fox—my mother opened it. On my return from school that day, she greeted me, all four pages in her trembling hand. It was no good lying or denying, or trying to explain. Everything was there. The lies I'd told for years. The gross humiliation of the disaster. I said I was sorry.

And I was.

* * *

I had developed a tremendous crush

on the British actor, Roland Blythe, then gracing the Odéon in a long run of Shakespearean roles, for which he was famous. A short, burly man, not conventionally beautiful, Roland's mouth was fleshy, but he had a thin patrician nose and a noble brow. (Too much brow; he wore a perfectly matched hairpiece to conceal how past his prime he was.) But his voice never deserted him; he had a voice like sounding trumpets, and beaten gold. So powerful a performer was he that some years before, a London critic had dubbed him 'The Soul of Conviction.' The Soul of Conviction had an unruly prick. Roland was the co-respondent in divorce suits all over the world, and even when I met him, in his fifties, a breaker of hearts. His musky attraction to women was part of his powerful charm, and he played it for all it was worth.

I was a budding girl, kneeling at his feet, sewing a torn bit of false ermine on his kingly robes for Lear when he one day reached down and took my chin in his hands and turned my face to his. His false beard beaded with sweat and make up glowed all over his face. He said to me, 'What is your name, child?'

'Audra Fox,' said I.

'Music,' he said, speaking with the soul of conviction, and looking high up into the flies. 'Audra is music. Fox must go.'

Susan kneeling behind him gave him a great prick with a needle. He yelped at the sting of it and turned to her angrily, but she continued sewing at his feet, and did not look up. When he returned to the stage, she shook her finger at me.

Roland must have been jaded beyond all desire, or sick with surfeit because he continued to pursue me, if the phrase is not too ridiculous in these circumstances, a man in his fifties, a girl in her teens. Now, I can imagine that we—Audra the lovesick maiden, Roland, the smitten swain—were the laughingstock of the Odéon. Everyone must have watched and chortled. (Everyone except for Mr. Crudup. In his presence the entire crew and company, even someone as illustrious as Roland Blythe, were prim as Presbyterians.) Susan knew; angry grimaces would play over her face, and she would not let me tend to Roland's costumes. She kept her eagle eye on me, but a theatre is a vast place. Roland and I would steal kisses in the passages while he whispered hurried bits of love lines, mostly Shakespeare, against the shell of my ear. I let him take liberties. My nipples tingled for hours after he had tweaked and petted them. Though I did not tell him of my acting aspirations (we had little time for shared confidences) yet I saw my future with Roland, and his with me. I would offer him my youth, and he would offer me his experience; he would teach me, and together we would be great actors, Canada's much feted Lunt and Fontaine. Beloved by the Soul of Conviction, I was transformed, beatified, my very walk infused with new grace.

From the wings on those Saturday matinees I cast Roland long loving glances, though he was hideous in his Richard III garb, hump and all, and he was terrifying as the mad King Lear. These were his best roles. I watched him wreak his magic and applauded with everyone else. Then, as soon as I could duck away from Susan's gimlet surveillance, I would dash into his dressing room for furtive kisses, quickly exchanged before Susan would miss me. Roland had his own dressing room, and his longtime dresser, a man known only as Geordie, would be waiting to enter when I dashed out. At the time I thought Geordie must be pleasantly in league with our love, like a wee, wiry Scots version of Juliet's Nurse. But now I know he was just well-rehearsed.

On the day of the disaster, Roland was ardent in the extreme. There, in his dressing room, the lock clicked against intrusion, Roland's passion for me could not be constrained. He reached into my soul, and also, it must be added, under my blouse and up my skirt. I told him I had to go, that Susan would miss me. She would be angry, and I dare not He flung me hard against the wall and his fleshy lips parted, his tongue seeking mine.

'Tell me what you want, Audra,' he panted, 'tell me and I'll do it.' He said he was my slave. So intense, so rich was his golden voice, so ripe with desire, that I gasped, and clung to him and the specter of Susan Butterfield's wrath dimmed. His hands reached down and gripped my buttocks, his meaty finger prodded between my legs, under and into my underpants. 'Tell me what you want,' he said over and over.

My heart pounded. 'A life with

you, Roland! The stage! To be an actress—' The words, my secrets came splashing out ecstatically with my love, '—to be Juliet to your Romeo, to be your equal onstage, that's my dearest dream, oh teach me, Roland. Take me with you when you go on to Toronto, Roland.'

In one terrible motion, he tore off my skirt, ripped my blouse open, yanked my brassiere off. He opened his Richard III robes and his great prick rose up before me. He planted his knee between my thighs, forcing my legs open, and threw me down on the narrow chaise (where, admittedly we had romped and fondled before,) but this time his great hands were not tweaking and petting my nipples, but twisting and grinding over my breasts. He thrust his full weight against me, and held me down. I cried out, not in love or lust, but sheer terror; this was not my ardent, teasing lover; this was a beast who pulled off my cotton underpants while he groaned and slavered over my neck, my breasts. I screamed until he covered my mouth with his, and buried himself deep inside my body.

I knew that I had got it all somehow wrong. I had confused love with death. Those dead who watched me from the dining room walls were watching now as Roland banged me again and again. I was dying. I screamed, I fought, I beat his back, I scratched his shoulders and shrieked. The dead were ingesting me while Roland pounded me into oblivion, and thrust his body up, through and into mine. He seemed to split me wide open.

And then, still heaving, grunting, glorying in his own strength, Roland held my shoulders down in a vise-like grip, and, in a coarse, wet whisper, he gasped, 'To —be—my—equal—?'

I cried out again. He slapped me a good one. I scraped my fingernails down his chest until he pinned my arms.

'I'll teach you to act!' he said, thrusting again and again, my head hitting the wall as he finished with me in one final furious burst.

There was a cracking sound, and suddenly above Roland's leonine head, I saw Fred Holliwell holding a fire axe up high. Fred tossed the axe to the side where it smashed into the makeup table and broke the mirror. Fred jerked on Richard III's humped robe and it came off; he pulled Roland by his hair, and the wig and the toupee came off, and then he grabbed Roland's shoulder, and finally Fred flung him back. Off of me.

I rolled off the chaise to the floor, arms clasped over my bruised breasts, feet pulled up in a fetal position, alternately whimpering and crying hysterically, choking. I saw Susan loom over me. A quizzical cruel expression twisted her mouth and her blue eyes had narrowed to slits. 'Susan, Susan,' I whimpered. 'He . . .' I wept the more piteously because I could tell from the look on her face that she didn't understand what had happened. Then she slapped my face. A single emphatic, wordless smack, harder, harsher than the one Roland had dealt. It snapped my neck, and took my breath away.

'Shut up,' she said.

'Oh Susan! Susan? He—'

She slapped me again. Twice. I tasted blood at the corner of my lip. I shut up.

Silently Susan started picking up clothing lying about the dirty dressing room floor. Fred stood beside Roland, axe in hand, as if expecting further trouble.

Roland was grotesque beyond belief, his great prick hanging limp and wet and spent, his chest scratched and bloody, make up running all over his face, both his wig and his toupee gone, his wispy hair all sweaty, the false beard hanging off his chin. Gasping, he reached with trembling hands for a cigarette. He fumbled among the shards of broken mirror on the dressing table for a match. He lit the cigarette. 'So Audra, you want to be an actress, you little whore. You are not ready. You need some experience. Some suffering.'

'Now sir,' Fred said, 'We don't want no trouble with the girl.'

Roland laughed, a booming, theatrical, insincere laugh. 'You want to be my equal! My partner on the stage? Don't make me laugh. You need to suffer. When you've suffered enough to play Mrs. Lear, you can act. And not before.' He spoke with the soul of conviction. 'You will be grateful to me for this, Audra. You will be.'

I sobbed and gasped. I beseeched Susan with my eyes, but she only raised her hand as though to strike me again. I swallowed my tears and cringed against the wall.

'When you've really suffered, then you can act, you teasing whore. Cunt. You're all cunts.'

'Shut up now, sir,' said Fred.

Spittle sprayed from Roland's lips. He drew heavily on his cigarette. His voice rose to a mincing falsetto. '*I want to be an actress. My dearest dream, oh teach me, Roland,*' he added, his mockery more painful than the outrage he had perpetrated on my body. 'When you're ready to play Mrs. Lear, you can act opposite me! But you will never, never be my equal.'

He snatched a robe off a hook, turned and strode out of the dressing room, and when he was no longer filling up my vision I could see a crowd of onlookers knotted at the door.

Mr. Crudup elbowed his way through these people, swearing at everyone, everything, the universe. He looked down at me. I cowered against the wall, covering my breasts with my arms, my knees drawn up, my buttocks bare. He gave Susan a brutal look too. He told her to get me dressed, to bring me to the office when she was done. He turned and left. He couldn't shut the door because Fred had cracked it with the axe.

Susan wordlessly yanked me to my feet, naked in front of all these people.

'I have to use the lavatory,' I whispered.

Susan rummaged through Roland's closet and found a dressing gown, flung it at me, and I put it on. She nodded brusquely to one of the young actresses near the door, and this girl escorted me to the toilet and waited for me, popping a blackhead in the mirror while I did my business in the stall. There was blood. And pee. And tears. There was something else too. Sticky. The girl yelled at me to hurry up. I wept the more.

She walked me back to the

dressing room where the crowd still collected, murmuring among themselves. There was no privacy. *Rape*, *rape, rape*. They all remained, milling around the doorway, *rape*, *rape, rape* speaking in half-whispered bits that I was only seventeen, not twenty, as they had been led to believe. No one was kind. No one said so much as poor kid. *Rape*. They grumbled and muttered about what an imbecile I was to think that Roland Blythe would settle for little kisses snatched in secret. They laughed. They growled, complaining of the newspapers and the police and my furious father when word of the rape got out. They knew Mr. Crudup would tolerate no scandal. Mr. Crudup was God, and Roland Blythe had crossed Him. Roland's run was over. No new play was ready. What had happened to me, personally, was a collective disaster.

Within half an hour, while I hugged the dressing gown and

trembled, shivered and wept, Susan—in utter silence—sewed buttons back on my blouse, and attached the sleeve back to the shoulder. She wadded my torn underpants and tossed them in the trash. She handed me the brassiere with two fingers, like it was a limp, lifeless animal. She fastened my skirt at the waist with a couple of safety pins. The look on her face was steel-eyed malice, rancor, deep and murderous. Without a word, Susan dressed me like a department store dummy, buttoning up retail clothes that were too big for me. She found a towel and rubbed Roland's sweat and make-up off my face, the blood from the corner of my mouth where she had struck me. Fred handed her a damp cloth and she scrubbed my face, rinsing the cloth and scrubbing again, while I cried. She held my hair in a knot in her hand, yanking while she dried my face. Then she let go. At last she spoke, without so much as a tic or grimace. 'Go home. Shut up. Don't ever come back here. Take her to Mr. Crudup, Fred.'

I never saw her again.

Someone fetched my coat and flung it at me as Fred walked me to the office. I clutched the coat to my chest. *Rape*, *rape, rape* rang, echoed in the empty high vaults.

Mr. Crudup rose from his desk when he saw me. He came to the office door. He nodded and Fred left us. Mr. Crudup took out a handkerchief and gave it to me, told me to blow my nose. He turned me around once, and looked down at my legs and white anklets which were barely tinged pink with the blood that had run down my legs. 'It was nothing,' he said.

'My head hurts,' I began to blubber. I touched the top of my head where a bump was beginning to swell.

'There now,' he said, 'there's nothing on your face. Put your coat on.' He held the coat for me, then put a guiding hand, gently, it must be said, on my elbow and escorted me to the stage door. He told Walter Jenkins to call me a cab. He put twenty dollars into my hand. 'Do you know what this is for?'

I shook my head. I started to cry.

He pulled out another twenty, folded it with the first and slid it into the pocket of my coat.

'For the cab?' I asked, sniffling.

He took out a third twenty, and then two more. He paused, and then peeled off five more twenties. He put these in my coat pocket too. He patted my shoulder. 'It was nothing. Really. You'll be all right, yes? Yes?'

I wasn't sure what was nothing, but I knew he was handing me cues and I nodded.

'You're not hurt,' said Mr. Crudup.

I shook my head. I found I had no voice. Mute as Susan.

'You're a good girl. You won't

tell? No, of course not. You're a regular little trooper, you are.' Walter opened the stage door and Mr. Crudup pushed me out on to the step. The door bolted behind me. I blinked against the cruel sunlight. I had forgotten it was daytime.

* * *

In 1957 I played Juliet for the first time. I had been an actress for several years by that time, supporting roles, bits of this and that, but Juliet! Nothing could diminish my satisfaction, my elation, not even that I was with a touring company funded (just barely) by the provincial government. We took Shakespeare to the benighted audiences of the Northwest Territories and the Yukon, playing in school halls, in gyms and cafeterias filled with great bearded males, a smattering of wives and pale, fat children, all of whom wore flannel. Never mind: I played the immortal role. I spoke Juliet's deathless lines.

On that tour I was supposed to be rooming with another girl, but I was sleeping with Romeo instead. (Truly, it did improve the play, though the affair did not survive the tour. There were Romeos before and after him, one true love, and three husbands.) The company traveled in a big bus that smelled of stale cigarettes and beer, though the discomforts are less vivid in my memory than the antics, the practical jokes, the card games, and good times. Oh yes, and Gordon Freeman was on that bus, as well, at the back, pecking away on his little typewriter, writing what would become his first great West End hit. Gordon played Juliet's father, and he was sleeping with the Nurse.

Our digs on this tour were usually old, drafty boarding houses dating back half a century to the Gold Rush, or cinder-block motels between a gas station and roadhouse (you could not call them restaurants). One morning Romeo and I, bundled to the teeth and cursing the Yukon cold, trudged from the motel to the roadhouse for breakfast with the others. The roadhouse coffee (and the mug that it came in) could have survived Hiroshima. Gordon remarked that we were safe from the Bomb up here, that neither the Russians nor the Americans could possibly want the Yukon. They all started off on Cold War fantasies and I went to the toilet.

While I was waiting for the single stall, I found a stack of newspapers on a chair, among which there was a two month old copy of the New York *Times.* It seemed to me a very pennant of civilization and I read every word, including the obit for the great Roland Blythe, an actor once dubbed the 'Soul of Conviction,' who had died in a Blackpool hotel, the death reported by a young chambermaid who had been turning more than his bedsheets. He died, apparently, in the act, and not the act on stage. I got teary. I don't know why. I could not help myself. I certainly hadn't any reason to mourn him, but neither could I despise him unless I were prepared to despise myself.

When I rejoined the others, I tossed out word of his death lightly, and we all rather chuckled at him, and his pathetic end. By that time I'd been acting long enough to share the theatre's wry, cold contempt for all those so-called 'great' actors. In public venues, we all spew effusion and respect. But in private? Everyone scoffs. The Soul of Conviction? The very majesty of the sobriquet curdles into cruel jest. That sterling title bestowed by a smarmy critic was the end of Roland's career as an actor and the beginning of his career as a joke. Roland Blythe's decline was well in progress by the time he met me. Professional jealousies, his advancing age and diminishing looks, sagging paunch, balding brow, his already out-dated mannerisms, (he'd made his stage debut in 1925!) these all made the great Roland Blythe an easy butt of jokes. But the incident with a teenage girl in dreary Ottawa, had finished off his reputation. There at a roadhouse in the Yukon, the story went round; others had heard it, but the Apothecary laughed and told it again, how the Soul of Conviction became the Humpless Hump. That's how Roland was known, *sotto voce,* of course after he got caught raping a teenage girl in his dressing room when three men had to pull him off the poor girl; Roland's robes and his wig and his toupee all came off too. It was hysterically funny.

That was the first I, personally, had heard of the Humpless Hump, but clearly, the story had been going around for a long time. Everyone giggled. I took a long slow sip of my

Cold War coffee.

In fact, the Humpless Hump as a sarcastic description outlived Roland and his reputation. The Humpless Hump, as a descriptive term, is immortal. It clings still to any over-the-hill actor in the role of Richard III or any of those Shakespearean cliched heavies. I heard the term (and a version of the story) a few years ago playing summer stock in Edmonton. No one cares that Roland was the original Humpless Hump. And no one knows that I was the girl at the heart of the joke. Mr. Crudup had bought my silence, and I never told what had happened to me in Roland's Odéon dressing room.

For years, I could not fully articulate what actually had happened, what the incident had done to me. But I knew this, oh yes, even at the time: Roland Blythe had ravished me unwillingly. I refused to think of it as rape, even though I wrote that cringing, abject apology to Susan, even though I sniveled and wept when my parents confronted me. But I am in the League of Survivors, and anyone in that league will not be raped. Rape implies a victim. Albert Crudup's payment implied I was a whore. I'd rather be a whore than a victim.

The only person to whom I truly tried to describe, explain what had happened, was my third husband—the best beloved of all my husbands.

'Don't cry, Minnie. He was a beast,' said my husband, wiping my tears, pulling the blankets to my chin. (We were Mickey and Minnie to one another, little love names.) 'He must have been mad to think he could get away with it.'

'Oh Mickey, everyone knew.'

'Of course, Minnie. In the theatre, there's no privacy for your sex life. Especially for your sex life. You can't fart in the prop room without everyone smelling it all the way up to box office. And you, just a girl.

He was a dog. And anyone who styled himself the Soul of Conviction deserves to become the Humpless Hump, though that's sort of an odd description, isn't it?'

'What?'

'Well, he did rape you. You said—'

'Ravish, Mickey. I said he ravished me. I was not raped. I am no one's victim.'

'Of course not, Minnie, dear.'

'No one cared, Mickey! No one was nice to me. Not even Susan.' For the first time in my life I was prepared to part with the story of Susan Butterfield.

'What did you expect? You did them out of a nice long run. Admit it, if we were suddenly cancelled, the play and actors thrown out on the street, would you say to some teenage twit—not that you were a twit, Minnie—oh, you poor dear. No, you'd say, ballocks!'

'No reason to treat me like a whore. Crudup treated me like a whore. He gave me two hundred dollars and kicked me out. And Susan—'

'Did you spend the money?'

'What?'

'Did you spend the two hundred dollars?'

'Yes. Not then. Later.'

'Well, fine then. You didn't tell?'

'No. I told no one. I've never told anyone but you, Mickey.'

'Then you kept your end of the bargain, and no whore. Crudup bought your silence, that's all. There's no shame in that. You're a fine girl.' He turned out the bedside lamp. 'Who's Susan?'

But my confessional mood had withered. I rolled over. 'No one.'

He patted my hip affectionately. 'To hell with Roland Blythe, and his telling you you had to suffer before you could act. Sod him. You're married to me now, and there'll be no suffering on my watch. You're a damned fine actress, Audra Lear.'

‘Thank you Mickey. Goodnight.’

‘Goodnight Minnie. By the way, did your father ever find out?’

‘Yes.’

‘What did he do?’

‘Nothing,’ I replied. ‘Go to sleep.’

Like Cousin Susan, I could tell many stories, but I am sworn to secrecy.

The day my mother confronted me with my letter of apology, *Addressee Unknown*, she banished me from the dining room till my father came home. I’m sure she sent me there for its abysmal associations with Susan, and I certainly felt them. I heard my father come through the door and I heard mother speaking to him, handing him the letter. He, too, read of the whole grisly episode laid out in my own passionate words.

My father came into the dining room, trembling with shame for himself and scorn for me. He said ‘Well, this should teach you a lesson.’

And of course it did. But not the

lesson he supposed. I understood that Roland had punished me not for hoping to be a great actress, but for saying so. Roland might still have ravished me in any event, but my words drove him into a murderous rage. I wanted to be a great actress, his equal.

My father destroyed the letter, and gave me the same advice that Susan and Mr. Crudup had given me: shut up. I did. I never spoke of what happened in that dressing room. I never again spoke of my calling, my dearest dreams, not to anyone. I returned to the ordinary life of an Ottawa schoolgirl. While I lived with my parents, in their house, I remained patient and quiet as a spider, though I had nothing but contempt for them, for my school, my friends and the boys who took me to the movies or skating in winter. How easy it was to use my body for power over boys. I learned that swiftly, easily, well. I was experienced.

At the age of eighteen. I announced I was leaving Ottawa. I had applied and been accepted to acting school in Toronto. My parents went grim and disapproving, united in their opposition. They would give me no money whatever. They declared that the theatre was not respectable and had I not learned my lesson in that dreadful dressing room? Oh yes, I told them. I learned I am in the League of Survivors.

I had saved Mr. Crudup's two hundred dollars, and I used it toward tuition. I felt redeemed in doing so. I found work easily, and in the theatre. After all I was skilled with a needle, and I knew costuming. Dedicated to my calling, I attended acting classes and auditions. I shared a string of dreary flats with three or four other girls, young hopefuls. In these years we went to bed with men we weren't always fond of for the price of a decent meal or the hope of a good role. We endured privation we could later laugh about, and humiliation we could not. We held each other's heads while we suffered from morning sickness and we held each other's hands after abortions. These girls were my friends and compatriots and competitors. They were hopeful, but I was destined. Mine was a holy calling. I was sworn to secrecy, but I took that great prick, Roland Blythe, at his spittle-sprayed word. I went on the stage as Audra Lear.

Now, there's a name they don't forget.

* * *

In 1961 I was Gwendolyn in *The Importance of Being Earnest*, summer stock at a theatre in Medicine Hat, when I received a letter from Mother. It was addressed to Mrs. Audra Lear. That was a huge concession for my mother. She would never use my stage name, addressing her letters first to Miss Audra Fox, and then to Mrs. Ken Williams, the name of my first husband. Across these envelopes, I would proudly scrawl, *Addressee Unknown,* and return them to her. That she would address it to Audra Lear meant something dire.

And indeed, my father had died. Decency dictated that I go back to Ottawa and stand in the windswept cemetery with the ready-to-wear relatives, that I stay in my mother's house to be a comfort to her. Except that her letter had been forwarded. Twice. I had missed the funeral by two days. I was greatly relieved to think that Mother had already turned father's picture to the wall and then in less than forty days, he would be turned over and, like the rest of them, cheerful at last.

Enclosed with Mother's black bordered note, there was a newspaper clipping. The Odéon theatre was slated for the wrecking ball. It had been a movie theatre since 1955 when Crudup went bankrupt, never mind that he had slaved everyone in his employ for years. Times change. It was bought by a syndicate that fitted it up for films, and so, the old dowager lumbered on for a while, then closed, and now it was a fire hazard and a public health hazard. The land it sat on was more valuable than the theatre. It was slated for destruction. The date set for the wrecking ball was the very day of my father's funeral. Had I been there, you cannot doubt which farewell I would have attended. And which would have drawn my tears. Sometimes even the theatre does not endure, Mr. Crudup.

But *Earnest* was in its last weeks, and my husband, the actor, Ken Williams, was having an affair. In retaliation, I, too, was having an affair, but mine wasn't going so well, and I was bored and angry and took the opportunity of my father's passing, to get rid of my lover, and tell Ken I was leaving him, for good. I was returning to Ottawa to comfort my mother, and the marriage was over. I would not return to him. He said good riddance, and that was that.

I had not been home, or even in Ottawa since I'd left at eighteen, nearly ten years before. I had not even seen my parents, so profound was their disapproval of my career. But the cab let me off in front of the brownstone, and Mother opened the door, she looked very much the same, a little grayer perhaps, and I stepped into the unchanging and unchanged world I had left.

However, I had changed. I could no longer be cowed. For ten days I strode those dark halls, with a kind of crazy strength and aplomb. I was young and invincible. I had bested them all, those hoary relatives who once wanted to slide from their frames and kill me. I felt strong and fine, not like a woman whose marriage has failed, and whose affair has gone bad, but like a woman who has taken her fate into her own hands, decided her path, and found her destiny, who has survived and prospered. I had vanquished them.

One afternoon I answered the doorbell, and saw two men. I thought they must be paying belated respects to my father. But no. They had badges. They identified themselves as Canadian immigration and asked to speak to Mrs. Fox. Mother came to the door, and they inquired after Susan Butterfield.

'I know nothing of Susan,' declared Mother. 'Nothing for years.'

'But she lived with you for a time. When she first arrived in Canada.'

'Yes, but she left us years and years ago.'

'Susan Butterfield is your cousin?'

'A second cousin. Actually, I

had never met her. Her side of the family remained in England. My grandfather emigrated to Canada in 1905. We have been Canadians for generations.'

The older man, a Mr. McPherson, remarked on her patriotism, and she was pleased, and when he again asked for her help, she offered them tea. She introduced me as her daughter, Mrs. Williams, and asked me to show them into the sitting room while she made tea.

I ushered the immigration men into the sitting room where the television sat like a little fat idol with antennae ears and a doily loincloth. They each took a chair on either side of the idol. I lounged in the doorway in the manner of Katherine Hepburn. I wore a slim skirt, a tight sweater and pumps. My fair hair was in a lustrous pony tail, tied with a short scarf. The two men looked me up and down. I knew the look. I encouraged it. I was always amused to see how little a woman had to offer a man to get that look.

'What are you going to do to Cousin Susan?' I asked, lighting up. 'Deport her?'

'Yes ma'am,' said McPherson. He was dull and earnest, his gray hair crew-cut. 'That's exactly what we're going to do as soon as we find her.'

Mother bristled back in, carrying the tea tray; they returned their attention to her. They said Susan was living in Canada illegally, a fugitive from justice.

'And what did she do that was so desperate?' I scoffed. 'Did she kill someone?'

'Well, yes Miss, I mean, Mrs. Williams, she did. Susan Butterfield starved and beat her invalid mother to death.'

'Good God!' cried Mother. This was as close to an oath as she had ever uttered. 'That can't be!'

'I'm afraid it is.'

'Her own mother! That's awful! I

have a picture of her mother!'

I half expected Mother to jump up and run into the dining room and bring them the picture with the two girls and their be-ribboned frocks. Her hands shook, so I poured the tea, and we listened as in their repetitive officialese they described their mission.

Susan Butterfield should never have been allowed to emigrate at all. She had been forbidden to leave England in the first place. Though she'd managed to get out of Britain, she should surely have been turned back at her port of entry in Canada. But, well, in those years right after the War, there were so many immigrants, and refugees, and so much upheaval, and she was just an inoffensive quiet Englishwoman and her papers seemed to be in order. Canadian Immigration was not aware of her criminal record. Her name wasn't on any proscribed list. She had slipped through the cracks.

Wherever she was now—between the arctic circle and the Great Lakes, between the Atlantic and the Pacific—Susan Butterfield had to be caught and deported. It was 1961, more than a dozen years since she had illegally emigrated. However, they informed us, there is no statute of limitations on murder.

'It was a shocking case,' said Mr. McPherson, the older man, subdued and professional. 'Even in wartime.'

'Susan told me her mother committed suicide,' Mother sputtered. 'After that I never mentioned her mother. It would have been too painful for her.'

'No doubt, ma'am,' said Mr. McPherson. 'What did she tell you, Mrs. Williams?'

I was so unused to being called Mrs. Williams, I didn't reply at first. But then I came to myself and said quickly, 'The same. That her mother had a broken heart and wanted to die and starved herself.'

'Well she may have wanted to die,' said McPherson, 'there's no way we'll ever know about that. But Susan starved her and beat her. Her mother was an invalid and couldn't fight back.'

'That is unthinkable!' Mother cried. 'How could she?'

I knew how. I'd seen that look in her blue eyes. Inwardly, my composure crumbled, but as an actor, I did not betray myself. The woman who could strike the wounded? Oh yes, I could see Susan's poor old Mum, stricken and pleading for kindness; I could all but hear the old woman's whimpers, her cries, as I had cried and whimpered, that day on the floor of Roland's dressing room. Susan had struck her mother again and again until at last she shut up.

'I didn't know her mother was an invalid,' said Mother, her lips bloodless.

'She was injured that night,' McPherson consulted his notes, 'November, 1940. Her husband was one of the dead and her other daughter too. Mrs. Butterfield was taken to hospital, and treated for a broken leg, a concussion, and released to her daughter, Susan. They couldn't go home. Their house was destroyed. They had to be moved.'

'Susan never told me any of that!'

'And you?' Mr. McPherson glanced at me, alert I think, to my sudden discomfort.

'I knew that.'

'How!' Mother demanded.

'She told me.'

'What exactly did she tell you, Mrs. Williams? Can you be more specific?' McPherson studied me.

'Not much. Just about the bombs and the being moved, that she was alone in the world because her family and friends were all gone. Dead.'

'Well, that's true.' With the help

of his notes McPherson told us briefly the grotesque story. After their home was obliterated, Mrs. and Miss Butterfield were removed to an unfamiliar neighborhood where they shared a single room in a big house. They had a hotplate for cooking, but the toilet and the bath were shared with other displaced families in the house. People who lived there told the police the mother was never seen outside their door, though Susan emptied a chamber pot daily. Susan did the shopping, such as it was. They had no money. Everything rationed. They made no friends. The neighbors testified at Susan's trial that the Butterfield women kept entirely to themselves. Other testimony emerged as well: Mum's pathetic cries, her pleading. Oaths, whimpering that could be heard through the walls. Occasionally wailing. Then some ruckus. What kind? Well, not flying crockery or overturned furniture. Slaps, perhaps, thuds, more oaths. Then it would be quiet for a while. A few hours. A day maybe. Then more wailing after that, more of the same. Why didn't the neighbors knock and inquire after the old lady? A few tried, but none succeeded. A neighbor said she had met Susan on the stairs once and volunteered to look after her Mum if Susan wanted a bit of air or an afternoon to herself. Her offer was declined, and seasoned with epithets. Susan spoke to no one beyond what the neighbors described as a sort of grunt. And when McPherson said that, I could well imagine Susan's side of any conversation, her tics and moist little tongue perched at the edge of her lower lip.

Then, according to the testimony, whatever ruckus went on in the Butterfield bedsit, it ceased. Everyone minded their own business. Then there was no noise at all, but after a while there was a smell. And that grew more powerful.

My mother put a hanky to her nose, as though that smell wafted over us. Mr. McPherson stared at his cup. The young man with him crunched a dry biscuit.

'And?' I asked. 'What then?'

McPherson went back to his notes. The doctor who testified at Susan's murder trial said that Mrs. Butterfield had been dead perhaps a month, perhaps longer, when police finally entered the domicile. Susan put up no fight whatever. They arrested her and she went. The post-mortem made plain that Mrs. Butterfield had been systemically and cruelly starved by her daughter who ate the food from their ration tickets. Enough for two people. Certainly Susan looked healthy and well fed. Her very plumpness testified against her. Worse, said the doctor, Mrs. Butterfield had been beaten. Often. Her nose had been broken and two ribs were cracked after they had originally mended;

she was everywhere bruised. Never, concluded the coroner, in all his years had he seen anything so heartless. Susan refused to take the stand in her own defense. She didn't speak at all.

I'm sworn to secrecy.

No bloody wonder, I thought. Succor the widow and orphan indeed! Susan Butterfield would crush the weak, kill the invalid and eat her rations. The League of Survivors. Could I have done that to my mother? I felt suddenly sick; guilt and chagrin roiled through my bowels, and popped out in beads of sweat across my brow. Of course Susan's dribbling eccentricities had congealed into violence. That was the woman who had struck me across the face. I would never forget the force of that blow. I would never forget the look in her eyes.

'It was a different time,' said Mr. McPherson, old enough, clearly, to have been a soldier himself. He explained, that during the War, the judge, the jury would not have been insensitive to Susan's losses. The deaths she had endured: the two brothers, the sweetheart, the father, and sister, the neighbor boys, the bombing of Coventry, the firestorms. The city so destroyed. And then to be bureaucratically moved to a strange place. 'And let us not forget the very real threat of the Germans invading Britain. Better minds than Susan's had come unhinged. She was found guilty, but they didn't even send her to a proper prison. Susan Butterfield was sent to an asylum for the criminally insane in Staffordshire.'

My Staffordshire teacup rattled in its saucer and I put it on the table. I saw in my mind's eye, Susan turning over her saucer. *I came from there.* Staffordshire.

After a few years, McPherson went on, Susan seemed rather normal. She was never violent. She had given up talking for the most part, but that wasn't a crime, was it? She could communicate when she needed to. By 1948 lots of people, even the sane, were slowly emerging from their fears, their nightmares; the whole populace slowly sloughing off their demons. Doctors and staff assessing the inmates concluded that Susan Butterfield had been unhinged during the War by civilian suffering. Her release was also no doubt made possible because the Staffordshire asylum, built in 1873, was going to be torn down. She was deemed harmless, and given a one way ticket to Coventry where she had indicated she still had family. But since no one expected her in Coventry, no one missed her when she didn't show up. Against all the terms and provisions of her release, she left Britain almost immediately, one of the great ships out of Liverpool.

McPherson asked Mother, 'Did you know she was coming? Did she write to you? I have copies of her forms here and she has Mrs. Thomas Fox/Ottawa as her destination.'

'I had no idea she was coming,' said Mother. 'She simply appeared one day. I certainly did not know she was a murderer.'

'FOB?' The younger man asked Mother. 'When she showed up, was she FOB?' McPherson coughed.

The younger one corrected himself. 'Fresh off the boat?'

'I have no idea. I can't remember. She didn't say. She hardly talked at all. We did not know she was a murderer.'

'Did she stay here long?'

'Not very. I can't remember.'

'Three years,' I said. 'More than that. Three years and eight months.'

'That's quite a long time,' Mr. McPherson glanced at Mother, then looked at me oddly. He made some notes. He asked my mother, 'Were you supporting her all that time?'

'We helped her, yes,' Mother

stated. 'We did not know she was a murderer.'

'She was a murderer,' I said, 'but she wasn't a parasite. She paid rent.' Mother gave me a slaying look, just daring me to go on, and I did. Let's hear a nice fat round of applause for the League of Survivors. 'Susan got a job, and worked six days a week at the Odéon theatre where she was a wardrobe mistress.'

'The theatre they just tore down?' asked the younger.

'Yes,' I said. 'She paid my parents rent every week. In cash. She cleaned the house and did all the washing up and the laundry and ironing. She starched my father's shirts just the way he liked. She slept on the floor in the dining room and she never had a word of complaint.'

Mother said to McPherson, 'I'm not surprised she was insane. My late husband asked Susan to leave because she was making lewd gestures to neighborhood men. I knew she was a slattern. I never thought she was a murderer. I can tell you nothing more. I hope you find her and that she is punished.'

McPherson said the court would probably show Susan mercy, but she would still be deported.

'You will excuse me.' Mother rose. She took the tray and left the room.

I saw the immigration men to the door. 'I never would have guessed her for a murderer,' I said, 'but she did suffer terribly.'

'How exactly?' asked McPherson.

'Surely, after the story you've just told us, I don't need to elaborate.'

'What did you make of her, Mrs. Williams?'

My eyes met McPherson's and I addressed him like Portia imploring the quality of mercy that droppeth as the gentle rain from heaven. I was the soul of conviction. 'She presented herself to us as hapless and harmless and pathetic. We believed her. She was an accomplished actress.'

McPherson paused. 'Have you had contact with her in these years, Mrs. Williams?'

I lowered my voice to a moist, husky voice, rather like Lauren Bacall in *To Have and Have Not*. 'Why yes,' I said, wafting a silken whisper round my well-told lie. 'Unbeknownst to my mother I got a couple of letters from Susan, the last perhaps two years ago.'

'Do you have any of these letters?'

'No. I threw them all away.'

'Did you reply?'

'No. What was there to say?'

'What did she write to you?'

'Not much. The weather.'

'The weather where?'

'Alberta.'

'What was she doing there?'

'Waiting tables, I believe. Something like that. Washing up in a café or some such.'

'So she could eat,' laughed the younger man, quickly silenced by a look from McPherson.

'She was living in somewhere in Alberta,' I continued, 'and she was going under the name of Mrs. Lear.'

'Mrs. Lear. Odd,' he said, making a note and closing his book.

'All the world's a stage,' I replied.